Farmer Enno
and
His Cow

Farmer Enno
and
His Cow

Jens Rassmus

Orchard Books • *New York*

Farmer Enno lived on a green hill in the country. He had three fields, a vegetable garden, and a cow. The cow he named Africa, after the shape of her biggest spot.

One night, Farmer Enno had a dream. In the dream he was captain of an orange ship sailing on the open sea. Towering waves rocked the boat, and salt water sprayed his face. He could see exotic lands on the horizon.

When Farmer Enno woke the next morning, something lay on the floor not far from his bed: an orange boat—exactly like the one in his dream—but much smaller. How strange, thought Farmer Enno. How did it get here? He put it on the shelf.

That night, Farmer Enno dreamed again about piloting a ship across the sea. This time the ship was green with a yellow smokestack. When he rubbed the sleep from his eyes at first light, by his bed lay a small green boat with a yellow smokestack.

This became a regular event. Every night, Farmer Enno sailed over the high seas, and each morning the ship he had dreamed of lay on the floor before him. Each time, the boat was larger, and soon Farmer Enno barely had any room in his house.

One morning, Farmer Enno woke and looked for the boat from his dream—but couldn't find it. It's stopped, he thought, relieved. What would I do with so many boats? I am, after all, a farmer. He headed outdoors to tend his crops, and there on a field lay a boat as big as the house!

Farmer Enno was flabbergasted. The next morning, he looked out the window and saw another, bigger ship in front of the house. Soon his farm was dotted with ships of many kinds in many colors.

"This can't go on," Farmer Enno said to himself. "Soon I won't have room for my crops!" He said to Africa, "I'm going to the city for medicine to cure my dreaming."

"Good," said Africa. "I'll come with you, so you won't be lonely."

As they set out for town, Farmer Enno tucked the small orange boat under his arm. It was the first ship he had dreamed of. He would show it in the city to help explain his sickness.

Getting to the city took most of the day. Farmer Enno and Africa went straight to the nearest hospital. "I have a severe dream sickness," Farmer Enno told the doctors. "I dream of ships, and they appear on my fields. Soon I won't be able to harvest anything."

The doctors looked at Farmer Enno, they looked at the small orange boat, they looked at Africa, and then they looked at one another. "There's no such sickness," they said. "But stay the night. We'll give you something to calm you, and in the morning everything will be fine."

Farmer Enno got a bed in a big ward. Africa was not allowed to stay in the hospital. She grazed on the lawn in front, which was more to her liking anyhow. Farmer Enno was discouraged by what the doctors had said. They can't help me here, he thought. It was a long time before he could sleep. But finally Farmer Enno's eyes closed, and he dreamed he was on a marvelous ship sailing the Seven Seas.

He woke suddenly to loud cries
and found people dashing back
and forth. There, in the middle
of the ward, was the bow of a
gigantic ship. Oh, my goodness,
thought Farmer Enno. This is
bound to mean trouble! He
quickly pulled on his clothes
and ran to the door, where
Africa was already waiting.

"Hop on," yelled Africa, and they dashed away.

They came to a park on the outskirts of town and sat in the grass to catch their breath.

"How will it end?" moaned the bewildered Farmer Enno.

"I have an idea," said Africa. "We'll go to the shore. It's not far from here. If you dream of a boat there, at least it can float and won't get in the way!"

"Good," said Farmer Enno, and they went to the shore.

When Farmer Enno saw the blue ocean and felt the sea breeze, he closed his eyes and breathed deeply. "It's wonderful here," he said to Africa. "I'll sleep on the beach and dream the most beautiful ship yet. We'll sail around the world in it." Exhausted, he lay down on the sand and instantly fell asleep.

But that night, Farmer Enno didn't dream of any ships. Not even of a rowboat. He didn't dream at all. In the morning, he sat sadly on the beach and stared at the sea. Suddenly he exclaimed, "We'll take one of the ships lying around on the green hill at home and tow it to the water!"

So Farmer Enno and Africa went back to the farm. But when they arrived, the fields were bare. All the ships that Farmer Enno had dreamed were gone. And, in the house, everything looked the same as it had before the dreams began. Only the orange ship was left, the one Farmer Enno still carried under his arm.

"What shall we do now?" he asked. "Now that I've seen the ocean, I don't want to be a farmer. I want to sail the high seas, but the ships are gone."

"Don't worry," said Africa. "Sell your farm and buy a ship."

"Africa, you're right. I'll do it!" cried Farmer Enno, and leapt up. "What a smart cow you are! Let's not waste any time."

No sooner said than done. To his joy, Enno immediately found a ship he liked. And, a week after they had seen the sea for the first time, he and Africa set sail.

"Where should we sail first?" asked Sailor Enno, at the helm.

"I have a suggestion," said Africa.

Sailor Enno didn't dream of ships again, not even of a teeny tiny boat. He was in high spirits as he and Africa slowly sailed toward the horizon. But a strange sickness was spreading throughout the city. . . .

Orchard Books, 95 Madison Avenue, New York, NY 10016

Manufactured in Belgium. Book design by Mina Greenstein.
The text of this book is set in 20 point ITC Clearface.
The illustrations are oil paint.
1 3 5 7 9 10 8 6 4 2

Library of Congress Cataloging-in-Publication Data
Rassmus, Jens.
[Bauer Enno und seine Kuh Afrika. English]
Farmer Enno and his cow / by Jens Rassmus.—1st American ed.
p. cm.
Summary: Farmer Enno is perplexed when the ships he dreams of sailing
begin to appear on his farm.
ISBN 0-531-30081-1 (tr. : alk. paper)
[1. Dreams—Fiction. 2. Ships—Fiction.] I. Title.
PZ7.R184Far 1998 [E]—dc21 97-40437